Dorset Ghost Stories

Prepare to be frightened by these terrifying tales from around Dorset

By

Richard Holland

BRADWELL
BOOKS

Published by Bradwell Books
9 Orgreave Close Sheffield S13 9NP
Email: books@bradwellbooks.co.uk
©Richard Holland 2015

The right of Richard Holland to be identified as author of this work has been asserted by him in accordance with the Copyright, Design and Patents Act, 1988. All rights reserved. No part of this publication may be reproduced, stored in a retrieval system or transmitted in any form or by any means, electronic, mechanical, photocopying, recording or otherwise without the prior permission of Bradwell Books.

British Library Cataloguing in Publication Data: a catalogue record for this book is available from the British Library.

1st Edition
ISBN: 9781909914469

Print: Gomer Press, Llandysul, Ceredigion SA44 4JL
Design by: jenksdesign@yahoo.co.uk
Photograph Credits: iStock, Shutterstock and the author

CONTENTS

Introduction	4
The Two Most Haunted?	6
The Screaming Skull	12
More Haunted Homes	15
Haunted Ruins	28
Ghosts from Prehistory	39
Ghosts of Coast and Country	48
Haunts in the Towns	57

An antique map of the historic – and very haunted – county of Dorset. Shutterstock Marzolino

INTRODUCTION

Dorset, in South West England, is one of the UK's most beautiful and historic counties. It is a land of rolling hills, broad pastures, picturesque towns and villages and a spectacular stretch of coastline.

Dorset is well known for its Jurassic Coast of limestone and sandstone cliffs, whose exceptional fossil content sparked off the subject of palaeontology as a scientific discipline. However, these are not the only ghosts of the past to be encountered here. The county has a rich folklore, which includes some of England's most intriguing spooks. A surprising number of these date way back into prehistory: fossil-rich Dorset can boast Britain's oldest ghost, a man from the Stone Age.

Dorset's ghosts date from all periods of its turbulent history. They include Anglo-Saxons; monks, knights and ladies from the Middle Ages; gorgeously dressed Elizabethans; figures from the English Civil War and the Monmouth Rebellion; daring and desperate smugglers and highwaymen; and people from both World Wars. Celebrity ghosts include Edward the Martyr, Sir Walter Raleigh, 'Bloody' Judge Jeffreys and Lawrence of Arabia.

In addition, there are stranger and more frightening ghosts. Here can be found the infamous Screaming Skull, invisible giggling things, a phantom monkey, spectral hounds with baleful eyes, savage murderers and ghostly coaches which mean certain death to anyone who looks upon them.

By exploring Dorset's ghostland you will also be introduced to some of the UK's most magnificent stately homes, charming towns and villages and some of the most picturesque countryside to be found anywhere. I hope you enjoy the tour!

Sir Walter Raleigh is one of Dorset's most notable ghosts.
iStock

THE TWO MOST HAUNTED?

Athelhampton House, near Puddletown, is arguably Dorset's most beautiful stately home. It is certainly one of the most haunted. A magnificent medieval mansion, built in the 15th century, it is celebrated not only for its Gothic architecture but also for its Victorian formal gardens. Both the house and gardens are open to the public and in addition there are a restaurant, an outdoor theatre and a cinema to enjoy. As 'Athelhall', Athelhampton appears in a poem by Thomas Hardy, and has been used as a film location, featuring in *Sleuth*, starring Michael Caine, and in the *Doctor Who* adventure *The Seeds of Doom* starring Tom Baker.

The best-known ghost of Athelhampton House is 'The Spectral Ape'. An ape appears in the crest of the medieval builders of the house, the Martyn family. Their rather cryptic motto reads: 'He who looks at Martyn's ape, Martyn's ape shall look at him.' In the crest the ape is shown holding a mirror. For this reason, the Martyn family – who owned Athelhampton for several centuries – liked to keep apes and monkeys as pets. One of these suffered an unfortunate fate and haunts the house as a result.

The interior of Athelhampton House is connected by a number of concealed corridors which served as hiding places for priests during the 16th-century persecution of Roman Catholicism. One day a daughter of the house, distressed at being jilted by her lover, used one of these secret passageways to escape to her room unseen by the rest of the household. Her pet monkey scampered after her, but its owner was so upset that she failed to notice it and it was locked in. There it suffered a sad and lonely death from starvation.

DORSET
Ghost Stories

The Spectral Ape is said to have been glimpsed about the house from time to time. Its most common form of haunting is the mournful scratching sound heard from behind the panelling. The Cooke family have now lived in Athelhampton House for three generations. One of these former owners, Robin Cooke MP, affirmed: 'The animal's scratchings can still be heard, despite quarterly payments to Rentokil. It can't be rats.'

The Spectral Ape is not the only ghostly animal at Athelhampton. Robin Cooke also encountered a phantom pussycat. He told ghost researcher Andrew Green that he had been working in his study when he heard his cat 'padding down the stairway'. The cat had been ill and Mr Cooke was a little worried about it, so he went to check on the animal. No cat could be seen, however. Mr Cooke spent about half an hour looking for his pet but was unable to find it. Later that day, he mentioned the incident to his gardener, stating how pleased he was that the cat had recovered. He was startled to learn that in fact it had died a few days previously and had been buried in the garden.

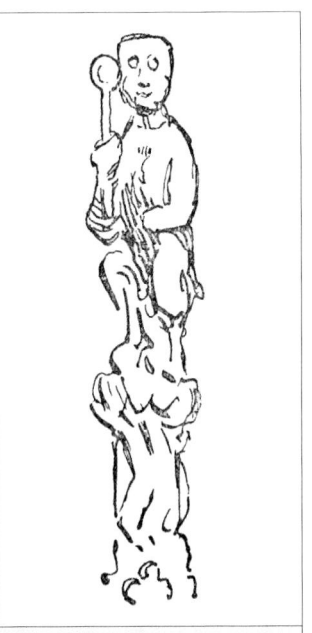

The Martyn family crest shows an ape or monkey regarding itself in a mirror. The 'Spectral Ape' is one of the ghosts haunting the Martyns; former seat, Athelhampton House.

The wine cellar is haunted by a 'phantom cooper', who is heard tapping away at non-existent barrels. Both Mr Cooke and his housekeeper, Mrs Chinchen, heard this phenomenon. A quieter manifestation involves an antique wooden crib. This is said to rock back and forth with no human hand to propel it. Paranormal investigator Jason Karl believes he saw this strange phenomenon for himself while taking part in a televised ghost hunt.

The most commonly reported ghost at Athelhampton House is a Grey Lady who mainly haunts the east wing. Her identity is unknown. One witness described her as 'wearing a full, plain dress and a gauzy sort of head-dress'. Mrs Chinchen also saw the Grey Lady, in the master bedroom. One night Mr Cooke was woken up in this room by 'a very strong glaring light' emanating from some inexplicable source. He also saw the door open and close of its own accord.

Equally anonymous is the apparition of a man in black robes and a hood. Possibly the ghost is of a priest who was resident in the house centuries ago and for whom the priest holes were constructed. The most dramatic ghosts manifest in Athelhampton's splendid Great Hall, one of the finest examples of domestic medieval architecture in England. The 'Ghostly Duellists', two young gentlemen in outfits of the 17th century, have been seen to swash and buckle furiously in the Great Hall. The savage duel continues vividly but silently for some time, until one of the men is wounded, blood gushing from his arm. Then – honour presumably being satisfied – they vanish. On other occasions, headless figures have been seen sitting round the long table in the Great Hall.

Vying for attention with Athelhampton House is the comparatively modest but beautifully proportioned manor

Athelhampton House is one of Dorset's grandest country houses and has numerous ghosts. © *Athelhampton House*

house in Sandford Orcas. The village of Sandford Orcas lies on the Somerset border, and was indeed within that county until 1896. It is an especially pretty village of old cottages constructed of the local warm, mellow limestone, which has a decidedly 'Costwoldsy' appearance. The manor house is built of the same stone and has barely changed in appearance from when it was built way back in 1530.

During the 1970s, when Athelhampton was also at the height of its ghostly fame, the then owner of Sandford Orcas Manor, Colonel Francis Claridge, boasted that his home was the haunt of more than a dozen ghosts. After writer Marc Alexander visited, he was impressed enough to describe the manor (in his *Phantom Britain*) as 'the most haunted house in England'. During his tour round the house, Colonel Claridge told Mr

Alexander about his own ghost sighting. One afternoon he spotted an unkempt-looking woman walking across his lawn. Presuming her to be a trespasser, the Colonel went out to tell her off, but as soon as he approached, the woman vanished before his eyes.

There are more phantom females in the house itself. The ghost described as being of 'a very nice old lady' only manifests when children are in the house. She likes to check on the youngsters as they sleep, but no one has ever been alarmed by her gentle presence. In addition there are the apparitions of a woman in a green gown and another dressed in red. The latter, who haunts the main staircase, appears to be wearing the ghostly facsimile of a red silk gown of the Georgian period that was found years ago packed away in a priest hole.

Talking of priest holes, a malevolent-looking priest haunts one of the bedrooms in Sandford Orcas. Another bedroom is haunted by a man in full evening dress, who is described as having 'an evil-looking face'. A third is troubled by the spirit of a servant who crept into the room when his master was asleep and murdered him by pulling a cheese-wire across his throat. A nice bunch!

Even more frightening, however, is the disturbingly physical presence of a brutal assailant of women. His looming, shadowy figure has been seen crossing from the gatehouse to the former servants' quarters. Once he arrives, the sounds of bodies being dragged about can be heard, as well as knockings on doors. The haunting, when it occurs, always takes place between 10 and 11 o'clock at night. One unlucky young woman was sleeping in this part of the house when the ghost arrived on one of its nocturnal prowls. She was hurled to the floor and woke to feel fingers gripping her throat. Fortunately, the terrifying experience was over almost as soon as it had begun.

From an obscure room at the back of the house unearthly wails have been heard. They are thought to be made by the tortured spirit of a madman who was kept locked up in the room for years. Another sad soul haunts the gatehouse, where he hanged himself centuries ago.

Even now we are not at the end of Sandford Orcas's spooky roster. Marc Alexander also learnt of several spectral monks in the grounds; the apparition of a man in the costume of the Stuart period, seen through a window; a woman in Elizabethan dress in the courtyard; a little girl in black seen at the foot of the stairs; and a friendly fox terrier which appears

Beautiful Sandford Orcas Manor has a good claim to be Dorset's most haunted house. © Mike Searle

in the Great Hall on the anniversary of his death, wagging his stump of a tail. The ghostly strains of a spinet and occasional poltergeist activity have also been reported over the years.

THE SCREAMING SKULL

Bettiscombe Manor is a sizeable farmhouse with Tudor origins in a tiny village in western Dorset. Even today it is rather remote, but for most of its existence there was not even a road to the place. For time immemorial a skull has been kept in Bettiscombe Manor. The tradition to explain the presence of this grisly artefact was first noted by a keen Dorset folklorist, John Symonds Udal. In 1872 he wrote:

'The peculiar superstition attaching to [the skull] is that if it be brought out of the house, the house itself would rock to its foundations, whilst the person by whom such an act of desecration was committed would certainly die within the year. It is strangely suggestive of the power of this superstition that through many changes of tenancy and furniture the skull still holds its accustomed place "unmoved and unremoved"!'

Bettiscombe Manor is one of the best known of a number of 'skull houses' in Britain. It appears to have been an ancient tradition to keep a skull in a property as a good-luck charm or protection against malign forces, a belief which might date back to Roman times or even earlier.

According to the tradition, the skull at Bettiscombe belonged to a servant brought back from the Caribbean by either John or Azariah Pinney. The Pinney brothers were ardent Puritans, who unwisely remained outspoken in their beliefs after the

Restoration of the Monarchy. Their punishment was to be shipped out as slaves to work on a plantation on the island of Nevis. This business of making British subjects toil alongside captured Africans is an interesting sidelight on history one rarely encounters. The Pinney brothers succeeded in escaping their slavery (unlike their black colleagues) and were able to make enough money to return home. The 'servant' one or other brought back with him may have been little more than a slave, for according to the legend he was very unhappy in England, and when he fell fatally ill he begged that his body be returned to his native land. The request was not granted.

'One has only to consider for a moment', wrote Charles Harper, the author of *Haunted Houses*, in 1907, 'the effect likely to be produced among the ignorant and superstitious peasantry of Dorset in the early years of the 17th century by the appearance of a black man in their midst, to see that here we have, without any more foundation than this simple story, the basis of a very fine legend.'

In fact, more recent examination has shown that the skull, or rather what remains of it – for it is far from complete – is thousands of years old and was almost certainly dug up out of a prehistoric burial mound. It may, therefore, have been present in Bettiscombe as long as the house has been standing. Not only that, but the skull turned out to be that of a young woman!

Facts have never got in the way of a good story, though, and there are further traditions of paranormal activity breaking out in the house when anyone interfered with the skull. One such incident supposedly occurred in the mid-19th century when a new tenant came to the farm. Creeped out by the grim relic, he threw it into the duck pond. That night unearthly screams echoed through the house, doors were opened and slammed by unseen hands and the windows rattled as if they were about to launch themselves from their frames. The following day the new farmer was told about the curse on the skull and he immediately waded into the pond and, with the help of a hay-rake, fished it out again.

On a subsequent occasion the relic was buried ten feet down in the hope that this would sufficiently muffle its screams. By nightfall, the skull had succeeded in worming its way to the surface again and it soon made its displeasure known. Every further attempt to get rid of the skull ended with it being reverently replaced in the house to restore peace to Bettiscombe Farm. Even as late as the 1960s, a farm worker claimed he was frequently able to hear the skull 'screaming like a rat trapped in the attic'.

The legend of the Bettiscombe skull inspired a classic literary ghost story: 'The Screaming Skull' by F. Marion Crawford. This was one of the American author's last stories, written in 1908. Along with other spooky stories, including the exceptional 'The Upper Berth', it can be found in Crawford's posthumously published collection of *Uncanny Tales*. 'The Screaming Skull' was filmed in 1958.

In his *Haunted Places of Dorset*, author Rupert Matthews mentions that Bettiscombe Manor was also haunted by ghostly footsteps, heard pacing an attic room after dark. We now know the skull has no connection with the unhappy servant brought from the Caribbean, but perhaps this restless spook does. Mr Matthews also notes that a 'phantom hearse' has been seen in the lane that passes the nearby parish church.

DORSET
Ghost Stories

Bettiscombe Manor, where a 'screaming skull' is kept.

MORE HAUNTED HOMES

Highcliffe Castle is a neo-Gothic masterpiece built between 1831 and 1835 for Lord Stuart de Rothesay, an important diplomatist and right-hand man to the Duke of Wellington during the Napoleonic wars. At one time Highcliffe was the home of Harry Gordon Selfridge, the American millionaire founder of London's Selfridge's department store. Situated on an eminence near Christchurch, Highcliffe Castle is managed by the local council and contains a museum.

Strange goings on have been reported from Highcliffe's library. A former manager of the house, Mr Mike Allen, recounted how one morning he was taking photographs in the library when he found himself forced backwards by an invisible force. The doors to the conservatory were thrown open and he heard crunching on the gravel outside, 'as if several people were running through'. He told Roger Guttridge, author of *Paranormal Dorset*, that the lights in the library were frequently interfered with. On one occasion, the room was found to be blazing with lights, even though they had all been switched off the night before and the doors carefully locked. On another, spotlights aimed at a stall in a craft fair were found to be pointing up instead of down, the change happening overnight and 'against the force of gravity'.

Others have found the basement an eerie place, unnaturally cold, where one has the creepy feeling of being watched by unseen eyes. There exists a stray reference in a letter from a former owner that Sir Shane Leslie, author of his own *Ghost Book* among many other works, 'met a ghost in the passage' while visiting Highcliffe Castle. Unfortunately, this tantalising line remains the only clue to what might have been an intriguing encounter.

Unlike Highcliffe Castle, Wolfeton (or Wolverton) House, near Dorchester, is genuinely medieval. It dates from about 1480, with Elizabethan additions and modifications. A house may have stood on the same site, in watery meadows by the confluence of the rivers Frome and Cerne, as long ago as Roman times. Wolfeton House is reached through a Gothic gateway flanked by massive round towers, more reminiscent of a French castle than an English country house.

The gatehouse is the main haunt of one of Wolfeton's many ghosts. This is a Catholic priest called Cornelius, who came to England from Ireland during the reign of the decidedly

Protestant Queen Elizabeth II. It was illegal to practise the Catholic faith at this time. The then owner of Wolfeton, Sir George Trenchard, was also the local Justice of the Peace and he had no choice but to have Cornelius arrested. He imprisoned the priest in one of the towers but kept him in reasonable comfort until he was taken away to be tried in London. Cornelius was executed in July 1594. Soon after his death, inexplicable footsteps began to be heard in Wolfeton's gatehouse, pacing the room in which he had been held. The unfortunate priest's apparition has also been seen, standing on the staircase into the gatehouse.

Gothic revival masterpiece Highcliffe Castle has a haunted library.
iStock

The staircase inside the main house is a notable feature at Wolfeton: solid stone and unusually wide. Its width encouraged a junior (and drunk) member of the Trenchard family to attempt a crazy stunt in the 1730s. He decided to drive his racing carriage through the front door, across the hall and up the stairs. Amazingly, he succeeded without breaking his neck or even injuring his horse, although I suspect his carriage was a little the worse for wear after tackling all those stone steps. Despite the lack of injuries, this dramatic incident is said to have created an equally dramatic ghost, with the entire scene being played out again from time to time, although silently.

About a hundred years before this adventure, another paranormal event occurred at Wolfeton House. During a formal dinner, one of the guests, a senior judge, suddenly sprang to his feet, pale-faced and agitated. He called to his servant to bring his carriage to the door and then bade a hasty farewell to his host and hostess, Sir Thomas and Lady Trenchard, leaving wonder and consternation behind him. Some time later the judge explained that he had happened to look up from his plate to see, standing behind Lady Trenchard's chair, a ghastly facsimile of Lady Trenchard herself but with a gaping wound in her throat, from which blood was gushing. The day after his horrible vision, he received the news that during the night Lady Trenchard had committed suicide, by cutting her own throat. This tragic woman is the third ghost at Wolfeton House. Her headless form wanders the corridors after dark, wearing a grey gown.

Tarrant Gunville, near Blandford Forum, is home to one of Britain's few vampire legends. Here can be found what remains of Eastbury Park House, an 18th-century mansion which, in its heyday, was the third largest house in England, only surpassed by Castle Howard and Blenheim Palace. The high cost of running such a vast home led to half of it being pulled down within decades of its completion and, largely thanks to an embezzling steward, more and more of it fell into disrepair until, today, only the north wing survives.

The unscrupulous steward, one William Doggett, is the ghost here. When the owner of Eastbury Park House, Lord Temple, eventually discovered that Doggett had been spending on himself the money he'd provided for building work and upkeep, he gave him an ultimatum: pay back what he'd embezzled or face imprisonment. The sum involved was considerable, however, and Doggett knew it would be impossible to recompense Lord Temple. Rather than suffer the disgrace of arrest and the hardships of prison, William Doggett took himself off to an empty room in the house and there shot himself.

Soon afterwards, rumours began that Doggett's unhappy spirit was now haunting Eastbury Park. At midnight a spectral coach pulled by headless horses was said to draw up to the gates, and Doggett's ghost to emerge from it. There was no mistaking his identity for he was still wearing the distinctive yellow ties on his breeches which he favoured in life. The ghost would make its way through the house to the room where he took his own life. The sound of a gunshot would ring out and then the haunting would cease.

Far from being treated as tragic victims, suicides were still considered to be criminals in the 18th century, self-murderers deserving condemnation. The bodies of suicides were usually banned from being buried in consecrated ground. Perhaps Lord Temple intervened, feeling partly responsible for his steward's death, but for whatever reason, William Doggett was

Wolfeton House has two ghosts, both of which recall dramatic incidents from the past. © Mike Searle

interred in Tarrant Gunville churchyard. When his grave was disturbed many years later during remodelling work, however, Doggett's body was found to be surprisingly well preserved, plump and rosy cheeked. This incident seems to have inspired the idea that Doggett had become not only a ghost after death but something even worse – a vampire.

By the early 20th century, it would seem, 'the credulous country folk' (to quote Charles Harper) went in fear after dark of the rosy-cheeked undead steward. His sinisterly smiling form was supposedly seen hanging round the ornamental gates which still survive from the days of Eastbury Park's grandeur. If the locals really believed in Doggett's vampirism (and there is no certainty that they did), they must have done so because of what they'd learnt from popular fiction such as *Varney the*

Vampire (published 1847) and *Dracula* (1897), rather than from any genuine tradition. Vampires as we recognise them today do not exist in British folklore.

Forde Abbey, south of Chard, dates back to the 12th century. It started life as a Cistercian monastery and continued to prosper for centuries, growing bigger and bigger until it was closed down by King Henry VIII. It remained empty for about a hundred years before being converted into a grand country estate in 1648 by Oliver Cromwell's attorney general, Sir Edmund Prideaux. The house has remained in a splendid state of preservation ever since, and is now one of Dorset's most popular tourist attractions.

The ghost of Forde Abbey, not surprisingly, is of a monk, possibly Forde's last abbot, Thomas Chard. His plain brown habit, tied at the waist with a short length of rope, makes for anonymity, however, and there is no certainty about this identification. At any rate, the phantom is a quiet one, pottering along the Monk's Walk – formerly part of the cloisters – or standing in the Grand Hall, gazing out at the garden.

Below the chapel is the family vault. In previous years the vault had a tendency to flood. One year, labourers working on repairs in the chapel fled, terrified, after hearing angry voices echoing up from the vault, accompanied by an irregular thumping. Later it was recognised that the vault had flooded again and the thumps had been made by floating coffins. One wag suggested the bad-tempered voices may have been those of the long-deceased Sir Edmund Prideaux and his son-in-law Francis Gwyn. In life, they had never got on and were constantly rowing. Perhaps, said the wag, they began arguing again whenever their floating coffins bumped into each other.

DORSET
Ghost Stories

Forde Abbey is haunted by one of the monks who lived and worshipped here during the days before the monastery was converted into a country house.
iStock

Apparently every inch the medieval fortress, Lulworth Castle actually belongs to the Early Modern Age and was never intended to be used as a castle. It was built in 1609 as a hunting lodge for Thomas Howard, 3rd Viscount of Bindon. As such, it must rate as one of the earliest Gothic revival buildings in history. Ironically, its high walls and towers proved the ideal place to serve as a garrison for a Parliamentarian force during the English Civil War, and briefly Lulworth Castle became a castle in more than name.

For centuries a private home, Lulworth Castle was gutted by fire in the 1920s. An intensive restoration programme has seen the striking building being given new life as a museum and a centre for cultural events, including Camp Bestival, a music-cum-arts festival. During its time as a country house, a puzzling phenomenon was regularly observed here. According to Antony Hippisley Coxe, in his *Haunted Britain*: 'For years a luminous spot on a bedroom wall withstood all attempts to remove it. Even rebuilding the masonry proved to no avail.' Presumably the devastating fire put paid to this oddity.

Equally misnamed is the fine Tudor mansion known as Sherborne Castle. Properly speaking this is the New Castle: the medieval Old Castle is now a ruin in the grounds. Unusually, the Old Castle originally belonged to the Church but was claimed by the Crown during the Reformation. This supposedly called down a curse upon its new owners: when the castle was gifted to the Bishops of Salisbury, it was intended to be for ever. The original deed included the words: 'Whosoever shall take those lands from the bishopric … should be accursed, not only in this world but also in the world to come.'

To an extent the curse could be claimed as having come true. After Sherborne Castle was taken from the bishops it was given to Edward Seymour, Duke of Somerset, a keen proponent of the Protestant Reformation. Not long after the Duke had moved into the castle, however, the young King Edward VI, worried by Seymour's vaunting ambition, had him executed. The king claimed the estate for himself – and died of tuberculosis the following year. The Sherborne estate next passed to Mary I, who suffered the same fate as the Duke of Somerset. Her sister, Elizabeth I, then took the throne and perhaps deflected the curse away from herself by leasing Sherborne, at a peppercorn rent, to the dashing Sir Walter Raleigh, one of her favourite courtiers.

Raleigh decided that the medieval castle was too inconvenient and old-fashioned for such an *à la mode* fellow as himself, so he set about building a New Castle. This grand house, with its staterooms and big, light-giving windows, couldn't have been more different to the gloomy old pile he'd moved from. Unfortunately, if there ever had been a curse on Sherborne Castle, then Raleigh may also have been a victim of it, despite his move. James I succeeded Good Queen Bess and he couldn't have been more different. James was a humourless, paranoid man who didn't at all take to the flamboyant, gung-ho Raleigh. Sir Walter was disdainful towards the new regime and when one of his treasure-hunting expeditions went disastrously wrong, the king took the opportunity to clap him in the Tower of London. Raleigh's men had killed a number of Spanish civilians in the Americas. Keen to keep in with the King of Spain, James I decided to rid himself of the adventurer. Raleigh was executed on October 29, 1618.

The apparition of Sir Walter Raleigh is said to revisit Sherborne Castle every autumn, becoming more active as the anniversary of his death nears. He is most often seen sitting at his ease on a stone seat overlooking the garden. Sometimes he is encountered strolling around the grounds, decked out in gorgeously coloured doublet and hose, a ruff at his neck and a fancy, plumed hat perched upon his curls.

The Digby family acquired Sherborne Castle in 1619 and have lived here peacefully ever since, defeating any further belief in a curse. In later years, Capability Brown laid out stunning new gardens around an artificial lake. House and gardens are now open to the public.

Sir Walter Raleigh is not the only famous person to haunt a Dorset house. An equally dashing figure from the 20th century, Lawrence of Arabia, is said to revisit his former home at Clouds Hill. T.E. Lawrence was an Oxford-educated

DORSET
Ghost Stories

The Tudor mansion known as Sherborne Castle is haunted by its famous builder, Sir Walter Raleigh. iStock

archaeologist working in Iraq when the Great War broke out. His fluency in Arabic identified him as somebody who might be useful in the British Army's campaigns in the Middle East. However, no one could have imagined the contribution this one man would make in the Arabian theatre of war. Lawrence's bravery, tactical genius and empathy with the desert tribes brought him success after success against the Arabs' common foe, the Turks. Lawrence's legend became assured thanks to a series of articles in *The Strand Magazine* and later through his own successful volume of memoirs, *The Seven Pillars of Wisdom*.

After the excitements of his war service, Colonel Lawrence found it hard to settle down. He joined the RAF temporarily, under an assumed name (such was his fame) and moved to

Dorset, where he lived in seclusion at Clouds Hill cottage, near Wareham. His few neighbours got used to hearing Lawrence's Brough Superior motorcycle roaring round the lanes; the only way, it seemed, for the war hero to get his adrenalin pumping. Then, in 1933, he suffered a fatal accident, one which has left behind it an intriguing air of mystery. Two boys saw Lawrence zoom past on his bike and, moments later, heard a terrific crash round the next bend. Hurrying to the scene, the youngsters saw Lawrence's crashed motorbike and a black van, which was speeding away in the opposite direction. The van was never traced. That night someone broke into Clouds Hill and ransacked his papers. Something for conspiracy theorists here!

Soon after Lawrence's death was announced five days after his crash, farmers reported hearing again the sound of his motorbike in the lanes. The sound was usually heard just before dawn. The witnesses insisted that the throaty roar of a Brough Superior was quite distinctive and couldn't be mistaken for any other motorcycle. Soon there were claims that 'a figure in Arab dress' had started to appear at the cottage after dark. Such was Lawrence's reputation, it began to be rumoured that in the future his ghost would only appear when England faced conflict or calamity. Similar legends have been attached to other heroic figures, such as Sir Francis Drake.

The cottage at Clouds Hill is now in the care of the National Trust. It has been left very much as T.E. Lawrence left it, and his personality, at least, still pervades the place.

About a mile from Clouds Hill is Bovington Camp, where Colonel Lawrence was stationed for a time. Bovington Camp is now home to a Tank Museum which traces the history of the armoured vehicle. One of the exhibits is a Tiger tank, and this is believed to be the reason why the camp is haunted by a ghost nicknamed 'Herman the German'. John Harries introduced 'Herman' to the public in his *Ghost Hunter's Road Book*. He wrote:

Colonel T E Lawrence, whose presence is said to still haunt his cottage at Clouds Hill and the lanes around it.

'At times he has been seen at the windows of the museum, staring out from the dark interior. The windows are high up in the walls and no one could stand there. At other times he roams around the camp, sometimes gliding in absolute silence, a figure almost indistinguishable in grey-blue uniform. Sometimes the ghost is invisible but is heard marching with heavy, measured footsteps along the paths of the camp.'

HAUNTED RUINS

In the previous chapter we visited a number of houses masquerading as castles. Corfe Castle, however, is the real deal. It is one of Dorset's landmarks, dominating the village of Corfe and the surrounding Isle of Purbeck from a steep hilltop. The castle was built in the 11th century on the orders of William the Conqueror to control a route between two hills. Its mighty keep was constructed in the first decade of the 12th century and although now in ruins, it remains an imposing presence.

Corfe Castle had a new lease of life during the English Civil War. The castle had become the private residence of Charles I's Attorney General, Sir John Bankes. When war broke out, Bankes stayed with the king at his temporary HQ in Oxford. Meanwhile, Dorset became almost entirely Parliamentarian in sympathy. The one tiny enclave was Corfe Castle, where Sir John's wife and children still lived. Lady Mary Bankes refused to surrender the castle to the Parliamentarians and it was immediately put under siege. The siege was less than successful, for the indomitable Lady Mary succeeded in swelling her tiny force of just five men to about eighty and was able to maintain a supply line of food into the castle.

A full-scale siege was now implemented. A Roundhead force of up to 600 men fought to breach the defences. But Lady Mary refused to be intimidated and eventually Corfe Castle was relieved by an army of Royalists. During the siege, a hundred Roundheads were killed but Lady Mary lost only five of her makeshift garrison. Although the battle for Corfe Castle was won by the Royalists, the war was, of course, eventually won by the Parliamentarians. Oliver Cromwell then ordered the demolition of Corfe Castle in what can only be described as a fit of pique. The Bankes family retained ownership of the ruins until 1982, when they presented them to the National Trust.

Lady Mary Bankes is one of the ghosts reported from Corfe Castle. According to Rupert Matthews, 'She is seen most often walking outside the main walls of the castle, gliding gently down to the stream that runs around the foot of the hill on which the castle stands. She walks with her head bent forward and with stately tread.'

The authors of *Haunted Dorset*, Chris Ellis and Andy Owens, add another ghost from the time of the Civil War siege. This is the apparition of a young woman who attempted to betray the castle to the besiegers and was later beheaded for her treachery. Her headless form has been seen near the gatehouse or wandering up the path that leads to it.

Other spooks date from the castle's medieval past. Ghastly moans and groans have sometimes been heard from the area of the dungeons. These are said to be made by the ghosts of noblemen who defied Bad King John and were left to starve to death.

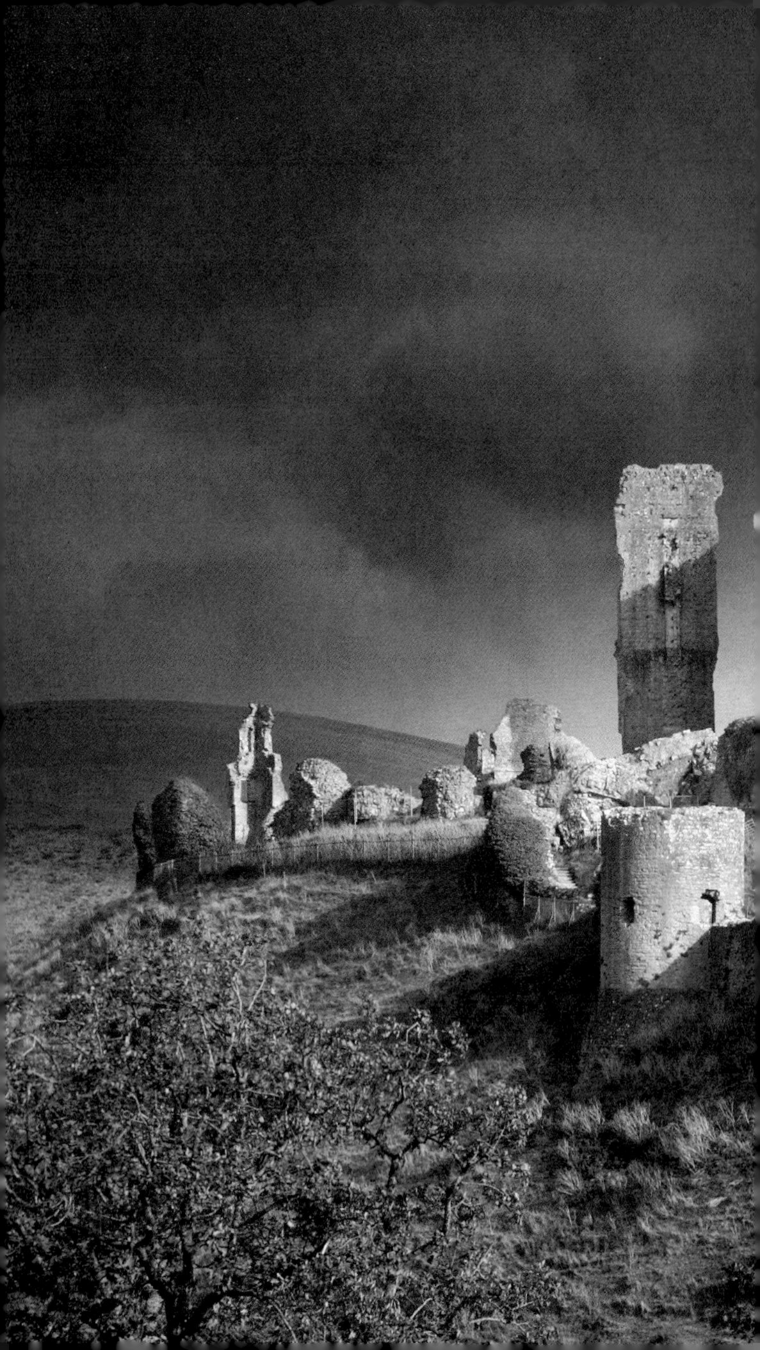

The ruins of mighty Corfe Castle are home to numerous ghosts. iStock

In 1973, one of the BBC's science correspondents, James Burke – the man who provided the Beeb's live commentary during the moon landings – hosted a special television programme from Corfe Castle in which a team of technicians attempted to test out a theory that stone walls could retain emotions or sounds from the past. This idea had been popularised the previous year in *The Stone Tape*, a spooky TV play by Quatermass creator Nigel Kneale. It is still known as 'The Stone Tape Theory' by paranormal investigators. James Burke and the TV crew came away from Corfe believing they may have managed to record snatches of speech from the castle's walls that sounded like English as spoken in the Middle Ages.

The discovery of Saxon post-holes on the castle mound indicate there may have been a large wooden building on the site before the Norman Conquest. This might, possibly, indicate the location of King Edgar's hunting lodge. In AD 975, King Edgar's eldest son, Edward, ascended the English throne. Edward had been born to Edgar's first wife, who had died some years previously, as had his second wife. Edgar left widowed his third wife, Queen Elfrida (more properly Elfthryth). Elfrida insisted that Edgar had wanted her son, Ethelred, to be king. Ethelred was still quite young, which meant Elfrida would have ruled as regent. Edward was probably only in his teens himself but was considered old enough to rule outright and received the blessing of the nobles, over Elfrida's furious objections.

The new King Edward is believed to have spent a lot of his free time hunting in the vicinity of Corfe Castle, possibly staying at the building which left behind post-holes on the castle mound. A nearby well was a favourite resort. Here the young king would pause to take a draught of refreshing water.

DORSET
Ghost Stories

On the morning of March 18, 948, Edward drew up beside the well and an assassin in the employ of the embittered Queen Elfrida jumped out of the undergrowth and stabbed him to death. Of Edward's murder one writer of the *Anglo-Saxon Chronicle* had this to say:

'No worse deed for the English race was done than this was, since they first sought out the land of Britain. Men murdered him, but God exalted him. In life he was an earthly king; after death he is now a heavenly saint.'

King Edward's ghost is now said to haunt Corfe Castle and its environs. Mysterious lights have also been seen floating round the well where the king was killed. On one notable occasion in 1991, a party of visitors to the castle distinctly saw a bright ball of light hovering in the air near the gatehouse. Highly intrigued, they went to get a closer look but the light seemed to be aware of their approach and it floated off round a corner and vanished from view behind some ruined masonry.

Edward's body was buried without kingly honours at Wareham and Ethelred took the throne. A year later the murdered king's body was exhumed so that it could be taken somewhere more fitting. To everyone's surprise, the corpse was found to be free from decay, a condition which in those days was seen as a sign of sainthood (rather than vampirism as at Eastbury Park House!). Over the forthcoming years, a cult grew around Edward and he became known as 'the Martyr'. Although Edward the Martyr has never been officially canonised, his divinity is recognised by three of the Christian churches.

Edward was buried in Shaftesbury Abbey. The scanty remains of the Anglo-Saxon abbey have been excavated and now form

DORSET
Ghost Stories

ASSASSINATION OF EDWARD BY ORDER OF HIS STEPMOTHER ELFRIDA.

Edward the Martyr takes a swig of water as an assassin prepares to stab him. The treacherous Queen Elfrida looks on. Edward's ghost haunts Corfe Castle and the nearby well where he took his drink. iStock the fabric of a delightful garden. A museum is also on site. The abbey grounds lie behind a massive stone wall on Shaftesbury's Gold Hill, the picturesque, steeply sloping street that is best known for standing in for 1930s Yorkshire in Hovis bread commercials. Gold Hill is haunted by the apparition of Edward the Martyr's funeral procession to Shaftesbury Abbey. It is apparently a grim and low-key affair. Two men are seen toiling up the steep hill, leading a horse over which has been slung a body in a sack – a very humble burial for a future royal saint.

Shaftesbury Abbey was closed down under King Henry VIII's Dissolution of the Monasteries. In those days the abbey was in the charge of a woman, Abbess Souche. Realising all the abbey's relics would be sold off, she was particularly concerned as to the fate of Edward the Martyr's remains. She ordered one of the monks to take the precious bones and to bury them somewhere secret. In the middle of the night, the monk gathered up the relics and stole away with them in a sack (much as they had first arrived). He was just in time. The agents of the Crown arrived shortly afterwards.

In the ensuing chaos Abbess Souche failed to learn where Edward's bones were buried. Hearing that her trusted ally was lying ill, she hurried to his bedside only to find that he was dying. The monk tried to tell her the location of the hiding place but was unable to do so. He took the secret to his grave. Ever since, his troubled spirit has haunted Shaftesbury Abbey's grounds and Gold Hill. One witness described him as wearing 'a brown cowl and habit'. She said: 'He came through the wall from the site of the old abbey, crossed the path and then just vanished.'

In 1931, during an excavation, the hiding place of Edward the Martyr's remains was finally rediscovered. A tussle then took place as to where his bones should be reburied. The arguments went on for decades, while the sacred relics lay in a bank vault. Due to complicated differences in theology relating to the kind of Christianity practised during the 10th century, and to the status Edward the Martyr has in their theology, it was finally decided the best claim belonged to the Russian Orthodox Church Outside Russia. They took the bones to one of their few British churches, at Woking Cemetery. This has since been renamed Edward the Martyr Orthodox Church and here at last the murdered monarch rests in peace. The ghostly monk of Shaftesbury Abbey is also able to rest now that the relics have been rediscovered. He is rarely seen these days.

Gold Hill, Shaftesbury, is haunted by ghosts associated with the burial of Edward the Martyr at Shaftesbury Abbey. The high wall surrounding the abbey ruins can be seen to the left of the picture. iStock

Even less survives of Bindon Abbey than of Shaftesbury Abbey. Another Cistercian monastery, it used to stand in a prominent position on Bindon Hill, overlooking Lulworth Cove. It too was disbanded by Henry VIII and a country house was built in its place. This house was razed to the ground during the Civil War and the site is now almost bare of masonry.

A romantic legend, part fairy story and part ghost story, is attached to Bindon Abbey. One morning a novice monk called Luberlu was sent down to the River Frome to collect fresh water. There he saw, approaching him across the water meadows, a beautiful young woman, her long blonde hair streaming in the wind. He stood entranced as the girl sauntered up to him. He shyly answered her greeting. Soon she had engaged the tongue-tied young monk in easy conversation and he was her slave from that day forward.

Not surprisingly, the boy's vocation was now shattered. All he could think about was the girl by the riverside. He would volunteer to collect water from the Frome whenever the opportunity arose and, invariably, the girl would be there to meet him. The novice's distraction did not go unnoticed. The abbot quizzed him on his lack of vocation, and on being told about the mysterious woman sensed that more was at work than mere boyish infatuation.

The next morning the abbot allowed Luberlu to collect water as usual but followed him. Hidden in the reeds, he watched the meeting between his monk and the beautiful maiden. When Luberlu at last, reluctantly, made his way back to Bindon Abbey, the abbot stayed in his hiding place to see what the girl would do next. He watched dismayed as the woman waited until Luberlu was out of sight, then stepped nonchalantly into the middle of the River Frome and sank beneath its surface. The abbot waited and waited but the maiden did not re-emerge. Clearly she was no mortal woman but some sort of water sprite!

The abbot later tried to convince his young novice of the risk he ran of imperilling his immortal soul by consorting with a pagan spirit. The boy refused to listen to him and the following morning rushed down to the river as usual. But the girl did not appear and he never saw her again. Somehow she must have known that her cover was blown and preferred to wait for a new victim.

The story has much in common with folk tales of fairy maidens who emerge from bodies of water to marry mortal men or who entice them to a watery grave. Here we have shades of Wagner's Rhinemaidens and of Keats's 'La Belle Dame Sans Merci', who keeps her chosen victim in thrall, 'alone and palely loitering', beside a sedge-withered lake.

However, the ghostly figure of a young woman, wrapped in a long cloak of grey or brown material, is said to still be seen wandering the same stretch of the River Frome. If this is the apparition of the same spirit, we must ask whether the abbot had got it wrong. Did the girl drown herself knowing that her forbidden love for the monk had been discovered? Is this why her spirit continues to haunt the place? Of course, we will never know.

At Knowlton, in the east of the county, there is another interesting medieval ruin with a haunted reputation: a 12th-century church abandoned long ago and now an empty, roofless shell. Legend has it that in the 19th century thieves tried to steal the valuable brass bell still hanging in the tower. It was so heavy, however, that they were unable to restrain it on their cart and, with a loud snapping of ropes, the bell tumbled into the River Stour. No matter what they tried to retrieve the bell, it remained resolutely submerged. In time it sank into the soft mud of the riverbed, never to be seen again. Nevertheless, it is supposedly still to be heard on stormy nights ringing sonorously from the depths.

Knowlton Church is also haunted by a fearsome black hound with glowing red eyes. Similar fiendish animals are said to haunt many counties in England. In addition, the tall, imposing phantom of a man wrapped in a black cloak has been seen striding about outside the church. Both he and the Devil Dog are believed to be connected to Knowlton Church's remarkable location – at the centre of a prehistoric henge monument.

Church Henge is one of a group of three Stone Age monuments which consist of banks and ditches round a circular or oval ritual enclosure. The church was probably built in its centre to tame the pagan forces imagined to be present here. The cloaked man is thought by some to be the ghost of a pagan priest, but he could just as easily be a former priest of the church.

We will encounter a couple more haunted churches later on in this book, but for now Church Henge serves as an excellent taster for the following chapter.

DORSET
Ghost Stories

*The ruined Knowlton Church stands within a prehistoric henge monument.
The entire site is haunted. iStock*

GHOSTS FROM PREHISTORY

Fans of the works of J.R.R. Tolkien will be familiar with the Barrow-wights, mysterious, malevolent beings which inhabit ancient burial mounds, guarding the treasures interred within. Tolkien's Barrow-wights may have been inspired by traditions once prevalent in parts of South West England. In his excellent *Folklore of Prehistoric Sites in Britain*, Professor Leslie Grinsell collected an astonishing corpus of tales associated with Britain's ancient monuments and in Dorset he learnt of the 'Gabbygammies', beings very similar to Tolkien's.

Referring to a Bronze Age round barrow at Ashmore (now destroyed), Grinsell writes: 'It was formerly haunted by Gabbygammies or Gappergennies who made strange noises which ceased after the barrow was opened and human bones found in it were removed to the churchyard and reburied there.'

The Gabbygammies were never seen and it's unsure what nature of being they were considered to be. They may have been spirits of the ancient dead or an order of fairy or goblin (the fairy folk often lived in prehistoric mounds). Perhaps they were entities conjured up by our ancestors, like curses placed on an Egyptian tomb.

When Grinsell, a professional archaeologist, was writing a book on the prehistory of Wessex, he was given a first-hand account of the sighting of an extraordinary apparition seen near an ancient monument known as the Dorset cursus. The cursus is a Stone Age earthwork which cuts through the countryside for an astonishing six miles, with numerous burial mounds appended to it. No one knows what it was for. During the winter of 1927–8, an amateur archaeologist from

Wiltshire, Dr R.C.C. Clay, had been excavating a Bronze Age cemetery at Pokesdown, at one end of the Dorset cursus. The experience Dr Clay had during this excavation, and which he later related to Prof. Grinsell, has become one of the most discussed and anthologised ghost stories from the county.

One night Dr Clay was returning from Pokesdown and proceeding in his car along the road from Cranborne to Handley, when about 150 yards past Squirrel's Corner he saw a horseman on the downs to the north-east, travelling in the same direction as himself. Dr Clay told Prof. Grinsell: 'Thinking he was from the Training Stables at Nine Yews, I took very little notice of him at first. Suddenly he turned his horse's head and galloped as if to reach the road ahead, before my car arrived there. I was so interested that I changed gear to slow my car's speed in order that we should meet, and I should be able to find out why he had taken this sudden action.

'Before I had drawn level with him, he turned his horse's head again to the north, and galloped along parallel to me about 50 yards from the road. I could see now that he was no ordinary horseman, for he had bare legs, and wore a long, loose coat. The horse had a long mane and tail, but I could see no bridle or stirrups. The rider's face was turned towards me, but I could not see his features. He seemed to be threatening me with some implement which he waved in his right hand above his head. I tried hard to identify the weapon, for I suddenly realised that he was a prehistoric man; but I failed. It seemed to be on a two-foot shaft. After travelling parallel to my car for about 100 yards, the rider and horse suddenly vanished. I noted the spot, and the next day found at the spot a low round barrow.'

DORSET
Ghost Stories

The round barrow where the horseman disappeared was on Bottlebush Down. Dr Clay subsequently learnt of another sighting of this remarkable ghost. A few years later, the archaeologist Alexander Keiller, famous for his excavations at the stone circle complex at Avebury, told Dr Clay that he'd heard that two girls, returning home from a dance along the same road, had complained to the police that they had been followed and frightened by a man on horseback. Prof Grinsell also noted that 'there have been other reports, from shepherds and others, of apparitions having been seen in the vicinity of Bottlebush Down'.

A Neolithic burial mound associated with the enigmatic Dorset cursus ritual monument. An archaeologist working in this area encountered a phantom he believed may have dated way back to the same period in which these monuments were constructed. iStock

A number of other burial mounds range the Purbeck Hills near Lulworth. A spectral army has been seen marching from Flowers Barrow towards King's Hill. A witness who saw the apparitions in the 1930s described them as 'skin-clad folk', implying that they dated from the prehistoric past. Others have described them as Roman soldiers, but they generally seem to be indistinct, like shadows in a fog. Sometimes they are accompanied by the sounds of 'tramping horses and men'.

The first recorded sighting of the ghostly company was in December 1678 by a local squire, John Leech, and five other men. Leech numbered the soldiers in the thousands and he and his companions distinctly heard the 'clashing of arms' and other sounds as of a large company of men on the move. So convinced was he that some sort of uprising had occurred, that he rode off pell-mell for London to warn the government. Meanwhile his brother sent messengers to the local militia. The countryside was roused and more than a hundred people later claimed to have seen the marching men. Nonetheless, they must have melted back into the ether at some point on their route, for they were no more seen and the panic – if not the puzzlement – was over.

A strange phenomenon is associated with the 'Bincombe Bumps', a series of prehistoric burial mounds ranged along the crest of Bincombe Hill. On winter's nights a 'fiery pillar' of orange flame has been observed shooting up from the barrows into the dark skies. The column of flame lasts a few seconds then ceases. No signs of scorching have ever been discovered on the hill top and the phenomenon remains an enigma.

South of Dorchester can be found Maiden Castle, arguably the most impressive Iron Age hill fort in the UK. Tier upon tier of complicated earthworks defend a broad interior which formerly housed a village of round huts. Maiden Castle was the stronghold of the Celtic Durotriges tribe, who were ousted by a Roman army commanded by the future emperor Vespasian. Artefacts of the final battle between the two cultures have been regularly uncovered among the ramparts, in the form of arrow heads and fragments of weapons and armour.

The Celts were forced out of the defendable Maiden Castle into the more easily controllable 'new town' of Durnovaria (present-day Dorchester). In the 4th century, long after the hill fort had been evacuated, a Romano-British temple was erected at its east end. It's possible that the fort had retained a small Roman force or that religious rites had continued to be performed here during the intervening period. It's unknown to whom the temple was dedicated, but the name 'Maiden' is no clue, for it is probably no more than a modernisation of the Celtic *mai dun*, meaning 'big hill'. The ghosts of Maiden Castle may well date from this later period. They are described as wearing togas, but are more likely to be Romanised Celts than members of the original invading Roman army.

According to Julie Harwood's *Haunted Dorchester*, a spectral maiden also haunts Maiden Castle. She is described as 'a beautiful young woman dressed in white, with long dark hair who scampers about barefoot'. She usually manifests near the main entrance and appears frightened, constantly glancing back over her shoulder, as if she is being pursued. Her apparition only appears during the summer.

DORSET
Ghost Stories

Within the intricate ramparts of magnificent Maiden Castle phantom figures wearing togas have been seen. iStock

Not far away, in a suburb of Dorchester, there is another interesting monument allegedly haunted by Romans. Maumbury Rings is all that remains of Durnovaria's amphitheatre. The vague misty shapes some have seen ranged around the former seating area are presumed to be the apparitions of a Roman crowd watching a gladiatorial combat. However, as Rupert Matthews points out, the apparitions are so unclear that there is little to support the ghosts' ancient origin. Since the old amphitheatre was used for public executions as recently as the 18th century, it's possible the ghosts date from a more recent period and are observing an equally grim 'entertainment'.

But back to the Durotriges: another of the Iron Age tribe's defended hilltop sites has a haunted reputation. Three concentric rings of steep earthenware banks remain of Badbury Rings, an isolated hill fort which, like Maiden Castle, was forcibly abandoned after the Roman occupation. When the Romans quit Britain in the 5th century, anarchy followed. Badbury Rings was reoccupied by Romano-British people because it was so easy to defend. A nearby ancient boundary marker, the Bokerley Dyke, was made more secure at the same time. Both events probably followed the encroachment of invading Saxons. For this reason, it has been suggested that Badbury Rings may have been the true identity of 'Mount Badon', the setting of one of King Arthur's legendary battles.

In 1970, archaeology students working in Badbury Rings suddenly found themselves surrounded by the sounds of a pitched battle. They could hear metal clashing on metal, metal thudding against wood, angry yells and desperate cries, and the tramping of marching men. On the occasions the soldiers have been visible, they have been identified as dating from the late Iron Age or early Dark Ages, which has led some to believe that they are no less than the ghosts of King Arthur and his 'knights'. In his *Hants and Dorset Folklore*, Stanley Coleman goes further. He writes:

'Legend has it the victorious Arthur reappears on the anniversary of the battle [of Mount Badon] every year … in the shape of a raven. He flies around croaking his satisfaction as he surveys the scene of his triumph, then off he flies, to reappear the following year.'

At Thorncombe Wood a few miles to the west of Badbury Rings, another ancient ghost has been encountered: a Roman soldier complete with big oblong shield and plumed helmet.

The entrance to the hill fort of Badbury Rings, which some believe to be haunted by King Arthur's army. Shutterstock/Chris Pole

Finally, we must consider Eggardon Hill, which dominates the countryside east of Bridport. Its southern half is scarred by the ramparts of another Iron Age hill fort, perched on the summit overlooking a steep escarpment. Eggardon Hill has a decidedly eerie reputation. The slopes and summit are haunted by two very different but no less sinister phantoms.

The first is the apparently innocuous form of a white deer. Anyone so much as glimpsing this harmless-looking creature, however, is said to be doomed to die during the forthcoming year. No less ominous is the huge, black hound which is said to roam the hill. With its shaggy coat and baleful glowing eyes, it is a close cousin to the black dog which haunts the Neolithic henge at Knowlton (see the previous chapter). Legend has it that the Devil himself hunts on Eggardon Hill. With an entire pack of fiendish spectral hounds, he runs down nightbound travellers. Perhaps it is these lost souls whose bloodcurdling cries and shrieks are sometimes heard emanating from the hill after dark.

DORSET
Ghost Stories

Animals seem especially sensitive to the paranormal presences on Eggardon Hill. Dog walkers have spoken of their pets becoming inexplicably agitated, staring and growling at things only they can see. Occasionally, they have run away in panic, only to be found hours later by their owners, miles from where they lost them, still shaken and cowed. Horses too have shied at unseen things or have refused to budge along the lanes skirting the hill, as if they were aware of something invisible to human eyes blocking their way.

Horse-drawn traffic would sometimes find it difficult to proceed near Eggardon Hill, for the reason outlined above,

The ramparts of the Iron Age fort on Eggardon Hill. The hill has long had a reputation for spooky goings-on. iStock

but cars and vans sometimes suffer too. Engines have a habit of suddenly cutting out, and electrics fail for no discernible reason. This irritating and slightly unnerving phenomenon most frequently occurs on the narrow lane connecting Eggardon Hill with Powerstock.

GHOSTS OF COAST AND COUNTRY

We have already made several visits to the hills above Lulworth Cove, but the beach itself is haunted too. Lulworth Cove and the nearby Durdle Door natural arch together form Dorset's most recognisable landmark. Lulworth Cove is an almost perfect circle bitten out of the clay and limestone cliffs by the sea. It has featured in numerous TV shows and movies as the archetypal smugglers' cove or simply as a beautiful backdrop for a period romance.

There are two ghost stories about Lulworth Cove, the first of which dates back to the Second World War, when the cove was mined and sentries were posted to watch out for enemy ships. A soldier was patrolling the cliffs one moonlit night when he was astonished to see figures dancing in the cove. It was impossible for people to be moving about on the beach in such a free and graceful way without getting entangled in barbed wire or setting off a mine. The sentry ran to get help but by the time he and his comrades returned, the dancers had vanished. Since that night, the dancers of Lulworth Cove have reappeared from time to time on other evenings when the moon is bright.

The second story dates from the romantic days of stagecoaches and highwaymen. In the 18th century, Lulworth

Cove was used by small boats bringing in goods from the continent, and so merchants would make regular trips to collect their wares. They would invariably be carrying funds to pay for their merchandise. One night a highwayman lay in wait alongside the lane leading down to the cove in order to hold up one of these wealthy merchants. He got more than he bargained for when the coachman refused to be intimidated and vehemently fought back. In a desperate scrap, the highwayman ended up beheading the coachman with a wild sideswipe of his sword. The headless coachman now rides his coach at breakneck speed from West Lulworth, down the path to the cove.

The distinctive shape of Lulworth Cove. The cove is haunted by ghosts gracious and gruesome. iStock

Another headless ghost might be encountered in Yellow Lane, near Loders. This narrow, tree-lined thoroughfare heads straight for the notorious Eggardon Hill (see the previous chapter). One night a coach was being driven at a reckless pace up Yellow Lane and the coachman failed to see the rapid approach of a low, overhanging branch. The unlucky man struck the branch with such force that his head was struck from his body. The sound of the fateful coach is said to still be heard rattling up the lane, and the grim form of a man without his head has been seen staggering about where the accident happened.

Phantom carriages and stagecoaches are a feature of the Dorset countryside. The 'Turberville Coach' thunders over an ancient bridge of the River Frome at Wool and spells certain death to anyone who sees it. Fortunately for most of us, the coach can only be seen by descendants of the Turberville family, although this might include quite a lot of local people even if they do not bear the family name, for the Turbervilles were resident in this part of the county for centuries. A similar apparition rattles down Ashley Chase, a steep hill crowned by prehistoric monuments, to the manor house at Kingston Russell. It too has a headless coachman and, as the postilion, a headless footman. Spectres of this type are known in Dorset folklore as 'Death Coaches'.

The Death Coach may also be associated with another traditional form of ghost, a White Lady, who haunts a wooded spot between Cranborne and Wimborne. She is described as 'a female figure dressed in white, and wearing a hood which covers her face'. If anyone approaches her, she rushes off, apparently pursued by the sound of 'a wagon and horses going fast through the wood'. The origin of this strange haunting is unknown.

Another White Lady patrols the old road leading from Charmouth to Bridport. She is another busy phantom, scurrying alongside the verge as if trying to outrun someone or something (another 'wagon and horses' perhaps?). The apparition of a tall man wrapped in a cloak has also been observed along this stretch of road but whether he has any connection to the White Lady is not known.

Heading briefly back to the coast, we move now to Worbarrow Bay, east of Kimmeridge. Here, two centuries or so ago, one of Dorset's many smuggling gangs got into a fight with Revenue men. One description of the Worbarrow Bay ghost is full of drama. A smuggler is seen fleeing along the beach, coming to a halt by the cliff that bars his way. No pursuers are visible, but the ghost spins round in panic and then twitches and writhes as if he is being riddled with bullets. Then he falls, and vanishes.

Further west, the Isle of Portland is one of the places frequented by the unearthly Tow Dog. The Tow Dog is the Dorset version of a weird kind of spectre recorded through the British Isles and generally referred to by folklorists as Black Dogs. We have already met with examples of the breed at Knowlton Church and Eggardon Hill. Although there are variants, Black Dogs generally look like huge hounds with black, often shaggy, hair and fiery red eyes. They tend to patrol lonely lanes and footpaths after dark. The Portland Tow Dog has the annoying habit of standing in the middle of roads in order to force vehicles to stop. Then, having glared balefully at the drivers for a while, he paces off into the darkness.

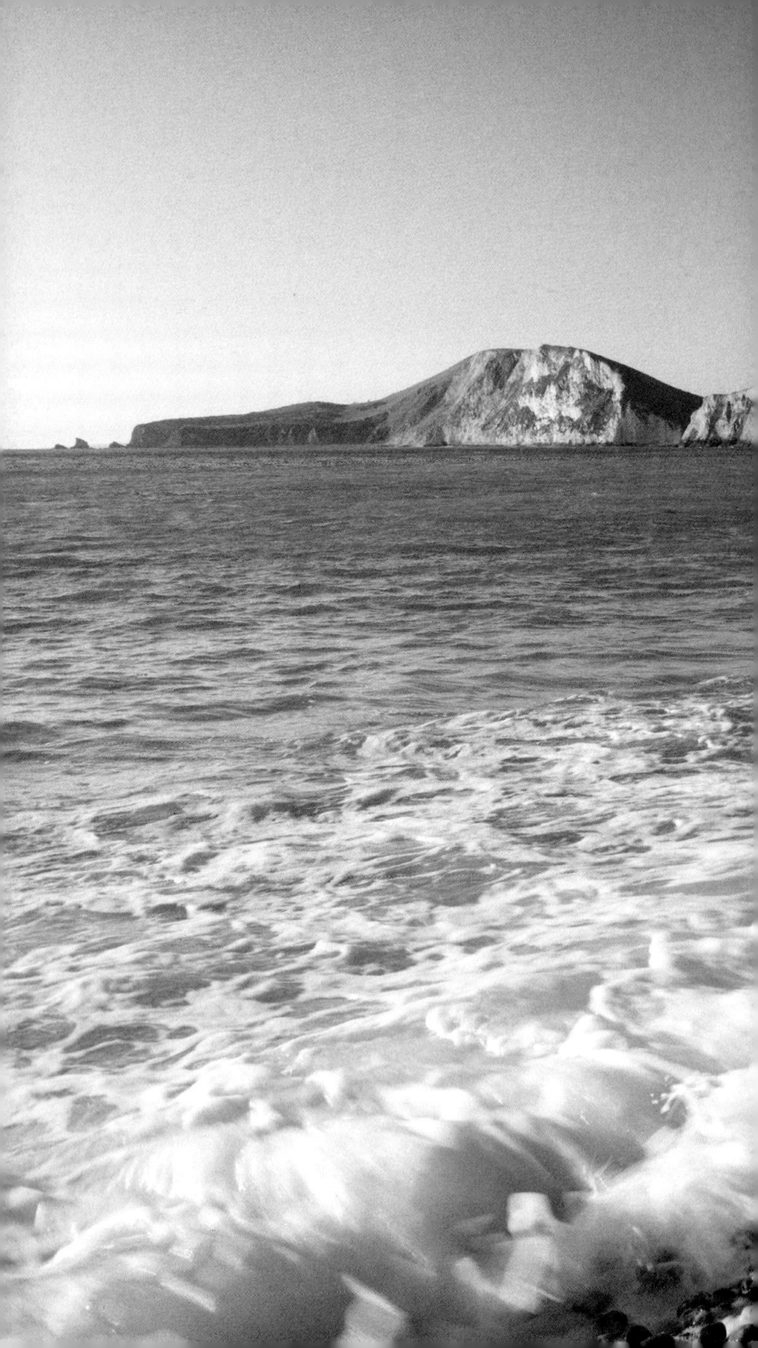

Worbarrow Bay is haunted by a ghostly smuggler, who died during a battle with Revenue men. iStock

Other haunts of the Tow Dog include roads through the villages of Chideock and Uplyme. The Chideock example would wait in the churchyard, sometimes patiently sitting on a tombstone, until someone happened to walk past. Then he would literally dog the footsteps of the passer-by until he was ready to faint with fright. An old inn called the Black Dog stood alongside the stretch of road at Uplyme where the ghostly hound made its appearance. It is thought many of the pubs around the British countryside are so named because they stand alongside routes patrolled by these wayfaring spooks.

Black Dogs and White Ladies might seem sufficiently weird, but the ghost of Cranborne Chase on the border with Wiltshire is stranger still. On December 16, 1780, a gang of poachers had a pitched battle with gamekeepers on Chettle Common. The poachers had been stealing deer for some time and the gamekeepers gloried in the chance to teach them a lesson. Nevertheless it was the poachers' leader, a Trumpet Major Blandford, who started the violence. He smashed a gamekeeper in the kneecap so hard that the man remained lame for the rest of his life. Another keeper sustained such severe injuries that he died shortly afterwards. However, the poachers did not have it all their own way. Indeed, they were so badly injured that the court took pity on them and their sentence of transportation was commuted to spells in prison.

Blandford was the most seriously injured. One of his arms was hacked off below the elbow. Such an injury would normally prove fatal in that day and age but he was carried to a nearby house and patched up quickly enough for him to survive. He was then gaoled, while the arm was buried in Pimperne churchyard (with 'full military honours' according to one source). Blandford moved to London after he was released, and was eventually buried there. Ever since, his ghost has supposedly been seen on Chettle Common searching for his lost limb. There is an old superstition that a spirit will remain restless if a body has been buried incomplete.

It has also been claimed that while Blandford's spirit searches vainly for his arm, the arm itself has also become a ghost. It has allegedly been seen crawling from Pimperne churchyard and through the lanes north of Tarrant Gunville in an equally fruitless quest for its owner.

DORSET
Ghost Stories

DORSET
Ghost Stories

The Isle of Portland is one of the haunts of the devilish Tow Dog. iStock

HAUNTS IN THE TOWNS

On Saturday, June 22, 1728, something extraordinary allegedly took place in St Mary's Parish Church, Beaminster. A village school held in the gallery in the church had been dismissed for the day and the boys were playing in the churchyard. When a few of them scampered back inside to look for some pens, they were startled to hear a noise 'which they described as that produced by striking a brass pan'.

At first they thought someone was hidden inside and playing a prank on them. Summoning their mates, they searched the church but without success. Then they all heard the clanging for a second time. Frightened now, they hurried outside. From the churchyard the boys could hear new sounds emanating from the empty church: a preaching voice and a congregation singing psalms. The sounds soon faded, though, and the boys rapidly forgot all about their strange adventure and got back on with the important business of playing games.

A little while later, one of the boys had occasion to re-enter St Mary's Church. He was stunned to see a coffin lying on one of the benches, just six feet away from where he stood. He ran to tell his friends and all twelve of them began to cram through the door to get a look at the grisly addition to the church furniture. The five boys ahead of the pack saw not only the coffin but, sitting a little way off, another boy, John Daniel. John had died seven weeks ago and yet there he sat, calmly and composedly, ignoring the hubbub in the doorway. All twelve of the boys saw the coffin but the majority were unable to see John's apparition because of the angle of the door frame.

One of those who could see the dead boy, however, was his half-brother. He cried out: 'There sits our John, with just such a coat as I have, with a pen in his hand and a book before him, and a coffin by him. I'll throw a stone at him.'

This final comment is so boyish as to have the smack of authenticity. The youngster lobbed his stone and the apparitions of both John Daniel and the coffin vanished. Word soon got round about the boys' adventure and they were all 'magisterially examined' (to quote the *Gentleman's Magazine*, which reported the incident) by the local squire, Colonel Broadrep. He was impressed by the consistency of their story, right down to the design of the hinges on the coffin they'd seen. This detail was later confirmed as being the same as those used on the coffin in which John Daniel had been buried.

Most impressive was the testimony of 'a quiet sedate lad' of twelve years of age who had only recently moved to Beaminster and who had never seen John Daniel. Nevertheless his description of the ghost tallied exactly with that of the deceased boy. Not only that, but he mentioned one detail his fellows had missed: he noticed a white rag tied round one of the ghost's hands. The woman who'd laid out John Daniel's corpse prior to burial later confirmed that a length of white cloth had indeed been wrapped round the child's hand and that she had removed it before he was placed in his coffin.

The appearance of the ghost set the rumour mill going. Why, asked the wagging tongues, would John Daniel's spirit haunt the living unless he had been the victim of some injustice? The boy had been found lying dead in a field near his home. His mother had stated that John had long suffered from seizures and he had therefore been buried without an inquest. Now people came forward with some disturbing stories. Two women 'of good repute' claimed to have seen a black line round the neck soon after the body was discovered, suggesting that John had been strangled. The coffin was dug up and the body examined by a doctor, who gave an ambivalent response to the suggestion that the boy had died of strangulation. The verdict was brought in that he had done so, nonetheless, but no action was ever subsequently taken against John's parents or anyone else.

Although John's ghost was not seen again, his mother subsequently began to haunt St Peter's churchyard. This does suggest perhaps a burden of guilt. Mrs Daniel's ghost is described as having a pale, drawn face and is seen wearing a long, dark-coloured dress set off with a bright shawl or scarf, and she has a broad-brimmed hat upon her head.

Dorset's county town, Dorchester, also has a haunted church. Just before Christmas, 1814, the vicar of St Peter's, the Rev. Nathaniel Templeton, had passed away. It was a busy time for the new vicar to take over and on Christmas Eve he asked the churchwarden, Clerk Hardy, and the sexton, Ambrose Hunt, to decorate the church ahead of the service the following morning. Hardy and Hunt were happy to oblige and worked hard making the interior as bright and welcoming as they could. After they had finished, they felt themselves in need of a little refreshment. This they accomplished by lounging at their ease in the vestry and helping themselves to a glass each of the communion wine.

This rather disrespectful behaviour did not go unpunished. Through the door swept the spectral form of the recently deceased Rev. Templeton, and he looked far from pleased. The ghost was waving its fists and shouting at the terrified men (although no words were audible). At the sight of this furious phantom, poor Mr Hardy collapsed in a dead faint. Mr Hunt threw himself to his knees and began to frantically recite the Lord's Prayer. Rev. Templeton's ghost turned away and floated off in a huff down the north aisle, and then vanished.

The phantom vicar has been seen on a few subsequent occasions. Each time, he looks decidedly cross, glowering down at whoever has witnessed his appearance. It's possible that since the incident of the communion wine, he has been unable to rest easy about his beloved church. Because the ghost cannot speak, it has never been possible to tell what has caused his unwelcome visits. For this reason, St Peter's Church may not have seen the last of the Rev. Templeton.

Dorchester's other famous haunting is linked to the Monmouth Rebellion, which began in Dorset with the landing, in 1685, of the exiled James Scott, the First Duke of Monmouth. The Duke was the illegitimate son of Charles II. When his father died, he was determined to take the throne for himself. The legitimate heir was his uncle, James, the Duke of York, but his Catholicism made him an unpopular choice for some. Monmouth exploited this anti-Catholic feeling to push forward his own claims and believed that a show of force would be enough to have the country rallying to his side.

On Charles's death, Monmouth landed a small force at Lyme Regis and immediately gained a strong show of support from gentry in the West Country. His rebellion was short-lived, however. After a number of skirmishes, it was soon crushed by the newly crowned James II's army at the Battle of Sedgemoor.

DORSET
Ghost Stories

St Peter's Church, Dorchester, is haunted by a former vicar.
iStock

Following the Rebellion, a top judge, the 1st Baron Jeffreys of Wem, was put in charge of trying rebels and supporters in the South West. Jeffreys was under orders to make sure no such trouble would occur again, and his response was merciless: hanging hundreds of people for treason, many of whom may have had nothing to do with the uprising. Many innocents found themselves swinging at the end of the rope during what became known as the 'Bloody Assizes'.

One of these assizes was held in Dorchester. The house in the High Street where Jeffreys stayed during this brutal time is a distinctive old building which now houses the Judge Jeffreys Restaurant. He attended the so-called trials round the corner at an inn called The Antelope and ordered the execution of every single person brought before him. He then had their heads stuck on spikes round the church as a warning to others. After the atrocity, it is said, the spirits of those killed on the Judge's orders returned to the house where he had stayed in search of him. Unable to find him, they still hang around, haunting the place.

Judge Jeffreys himself haunts the area where he condemned all these people to death. The Antelope Inn has long since been demolished and has been replaced by a shopping centre. According to Rupert Matthews, 'His figure emerges from a door that leads to the house where he stayed, turns left down the arcade and then vanishes beside what was the entrance to the room where he held his trials.'

Several interesting stories have been reported from Blandford Forum. In their *Haunted Dorset*, Chris Ellis and Andy Owens tell of a strange incident which occurred in the army base here. One evening in 1952 three young soldiers were startled to see a half-formed face peering in at them through a window

DORSET
Ghost Stories

The infamous Judge Jeffreys condemned to death numerous people in Dorchester after the Monmouth Rebellion and now haunts the town.

in their barracks. Its slit-like mouth opened and closed as if it was trying to speak and they could hear it scratching at the window pane. The thing moved from the window and slid off in the direction of the fire escape. One of the soldiers ran over to the door and was just in time to prevent it being thrown open. He used his rifle to jam the door, which continued to bulge inwards from the pressure exerted from outside. By this time the barrack block was in uproar as the rest of soldiers began to wake up demanding to know what was going on.

One of the original trio made a dash out of the barracks and ran to the NCO's office to tell him what was happening. Not surprisingly, the officer was less than impressed by the young soldier's panicky testimony, but just then an orderly ran in shouting that a faceless man had barged into the medical block and had started throwing stuff around. By the time the NCO and the two other men had rushed round, first to the medics' room and then to the barracks, the 'thing', whatever it was, had disappeared from the army base. It was not seen again.

A phantom steam train has been heard, though not seen, puffing its way along a disused railway line on the outskirts of Blandford. Oddly enough, a strange premonition was had by a former bigwig of the town, Baron Ryves, which might tie in with this ghost. In the 1660s Baron Ryves was dozing in his garden when he experienced a vivid dream in which a huge 'monster', breathing flames and smoke, roared towards him before suddenly veering off, pulling behind it a long, worm-like body. Cut into the body were a series of windows through which Ryves could see people sitting. Two hundred years later, Ryves' former garden was grubbed up to make way for the railway.

Moving to the coast now, where many of Dorset's largest towns are situated. In common with so many coastal resorts, Bournemouth only began to grow with the Georgian fad for sea bathing. The entire town was effectively founded in 1810 by entrepreneur Lewis Tregonwell, and it grew rapidly after it became connected to the rail network. One artefact of Bournemouth's Victorian prosperity is its grand Town Hall. It looks every inch the luxury hotel it started out as. During the First World War, the hotel was converted for use as a military hospital and its ghosts seem to date from this period of the building's life.

The apparition of a soldier wearing a uniform dating from the Great War manifests during the autumn months. He strides through the Town Hall's main entrance and then vanishes. On occasions a phantom horse is seen outside the hotel, and this may possibly be connected with the appearance of the soldier.

The other ghost of Bournemouth Town Hall is of a man in 'eastern clothes'. He may have been a member of an Indian regiment or perhaps had been a doctor at the military hospital. Or, of course, he may simply have been a guest of the hotel in more peaceful times. One witness to this ghost, a part-time cleaner, recalled:

'I had this eerie feeling, looked round and saw this dark shape moving towards me. It stopped only about six foot away and I felt a blast of very cold air. I could see plainly that it was a man dressed in eastern clothes with a turban. I could see that his face was kind of mahogany-coloured and he had a beard. Then, after a few seconds, he faded away like a film image.'

More commonly experienced than any of the visual manifestations are the inexplicable footsteps heard wandering around the former hotel. One witness, a young disc jockey, was setting up his equipment for a disco when he heard 'heavy clunking footsteps'. He went to discover who could be making them, but was unable to find anyone. Later on that same evening his promoter heard similar footsteps walking across the empty hall where the disco was due to be held. Night workers in the Town Hall have also heard the pacing footsteps on occasions when they have known they were the only people present in that part of the building. Whether it is the soldier or the Indian gentleman whose footsteps are heard is unknown. Perhaps it is neither, but a third, at present unseen ghost.

Unlike Bournemouth, the seaside town of Poole has been around since at least the 12th century. From that time its harbour became important in the medieval wool trade. It later developed strong links with the emerging American colonies and by the 18th century was one of the busiest ports in England. It was also one of the main disembarkation places for troops in the invasion of France during the Second World War (see also Weymouth, below).

Scaplen's Court is a rare survival of a domestic medieval building. Today it houses the museum service and a Tudor herb garden is attached. According to an old story, a horrible murder took place here in 1598. The owner, William Greene, died, leaving his widow Alice a legacy rumoured in the town to be as much as £200 (a lot of money in those days). Next door lived the mayor of Poole, and he and three other men decided to help themselves to the money that they knew had been made over to the widow. The broke in through the neighbouring wall and murdered poor Alice with a single axe blow to the head. Then they stabbed to death Alice's servant and killed a dog whose barking threatened to wake up the neighbourhood. Then they made off with the loot. One

DORSET
Ghost Stories

DORSET
Ghost Stories

Bournemouth Town Hall is haunted by a First World War soldier and a man from the Far East. iStock

member of the gang later confessed to the crime and was hanged, but the rest seem to have got off scot free.

The apparition of an elderly woman wearing a white apron has occasionally been seen about the place and is thought to be the ghost of the unfortunate Alice Greene. The sound of a barking dog, when no dog is present, has also been heard, and this may well tie in with the murder. A further ghost is of a man wearing a cloak and sporting a long white beard. He seems a friendly soul, however, and probably has no connection with the crime.

The Crown Hotel in Market Street also has a haunted reputation. The grim tale attached to the 17th-century hostelry is that centuries ago the landlord's wife gave birth to twins, both of whom were deformed. The landlord was ashamed of the children and kept them locked in the hayloft, away from prying eyes and the feared derision of his neighbours. For years the children lived a miserable life. Eventually, their cruel father murdered them and secretly buried their bodies. Ever since, the distressing sound of children's screams is said to have been heard in the Crown.

When the Crown was being renovated in the 1960s, several odd phenomena were reported. Three men staying in the hotel heard a single note played on the piano even though no one was near it. This continued for some little time. Later they saw what they described as a 'fluorescent mist' descending a staircase and crossing the courtyard. Since then at least two more ghosts have been observed here: a woman standing at an upper-storey window and the sound of horses' hooves clattering in the courtyard.

DORSET
Ghost Stories

Further haunted locations are listed in *Haunted Poole* by Julie Harwood. These include the Georgian Custom House, haunted by a smuggler; the Guildhall, haunted by a suicide and a murdered alderman; a former Seaman's Mission (now the Oriel Restaurant), haunted by an elderly sailor; the High Street, where several shops are bothered by a troublesome spook known as 'Jenkins'; and the parish church, where spectral wreaths sometimes become visible, commemorating all the fishermen lost at sea over the years.

Weymouth has been an important harbour and military centre since medieval times. Unfortunately, it is thought that the 14th-century plague known as the Black Death arrived through Weymouth, ultimately leading to the deaths of about

The splendid Guildhall is one of Poole's many haunted properties. iStock

DORSET
Ghost Stories

DORSET
Ghost Stories

The Cobb at Lyme Regis is the destination of a gruesome ghost dating from the time of the Monmouth Rebellion. iStock

a third of England's population. Weymouth was one of the first sea-bathing resorts in England, becoming popular in 1780 after the Duke of Gloucester built a winter home here. It became especially important during the Second World War. More than half a million US servicemen embarked from Portland Harbour to take part in the Normandy landings. The bouncing bomb was tested on the nearby Fleet lagoon.

An older remnant of its military importance is the Nothe Fort, built during the reign of Victoria to guard Portland Harbour. Heavily armed with cannon, firstly in fear of an invasion by the French, then by the Germans, the Nothe Fort's firepower was never actually put to the test. The invasions never came. In the 1940s rumours first circulated that the fort was haunted. A shadowy figure was frequently seen patrolling the walls, as if on guard duty. The apparition was never distinct enough to determine what period of the fort's history it came from, however.

Nothe Fort is now a popular tourist attraction. Over the years, its haunted reputation has grown and grown. Alex Woodward details a number of spooky encounters in her *Haunted Weymouth*. The author states that a young gunner, crushed to death by a cannon during the early life of the fort, haunts the subterranean passages. He is not seen but his surprisingly cheerful whistling is heard meandering through the tunnels. Lots of odd incidents have been reported from the old Shell Store: visitors have felt invisible hands touching them, young children have apparently seen people no one else could and dogs have become inexplicably agitated by an unknown presence. There is also a door in the main complex that likes to stay open, however firmly it is shut. In 1983, a boy who had sneaked into the then deserted fort clearly saw a pitch-black silhouette of a man crossing the parade ground. It turned and looked at him before continuing on its way. This may well have been a more recent sighting of the shadowy apparition reported in the 1940s.

Further haunted sites in Weymouth highlighted by Alex Woodward include: the Boot Inn, where the ghost of a sailor in jersey and big boots has been seen and sea shanties heard in empty rooms; the Black Dog pub, where phantom smugglers fight over booty disposed of centuries ago; Franchise Street, Chapelhay, where the sounds of a Civil War battle continue to echo; the Chapelhay Steps, down which men – but no women – have been pushed by invisible hands; and the Cannonball House (so named for the Civil War cannonball buried in the masonry), in which a ghostly old woman revealed the existence of a bricked-up room where a corpse lay. In addition, the ghost of a man killed by a railway train haunts Bincombe Tunnel and a phantom ship in full sail has been known to silently sail into Weymouth harbour before melting into thin air.

Heading to the west of the county, we come to Bridport, which started life as a Saxon settlement and later became the centre of the formerly crucial rope-making industry in England. Several ghosts haunt the town.

Squire Bright was the archetypal 18th-century squire: hard-drinking, womanizing and full of mischief. In 1748 he left his home, Baglake House, and came to Bridport looking for fun. He lived it up for several days and nights and then the unexpected happened. After paying a call on an unknown gentleman, whose identity was never discovered, Squire Bright returned with his enthusiasm decidedly dimmed. He was morose all day. Suddenly, as if he had made a difficult decision, he jumped on his horse and rode away without a word to his manservant. Anxious about his master, the servant decided to follow him – but too late. Squire Bright had ridden to the River Mangerton and had drowned himself there.

The manservant dragged the squire's sodden body from the river and then turned towards the town to alert the authorities. Moments later he was horrified to see the apparition of his dead master standing on the road before him. The poor man tumbled from his horse at the shock and never entirely recovered. The reason for Squire Bright's suicide remains a mystery but his ghost is occasionally seen riding down the lane to the stretch of river where he took his own life.

Meanwhile, Gipsy Lane is haunted by a Grey Lady. Usually, such phantoms are so named for the colour of the dress they are seen wearing – often they are nuns – but the Bridport example takes the name to extremes. Take the testimony of one person who encountered her (as quoted in Ellis and Owen's *Haunted Dorset*): 'A lady of about sixty years old appeared from nowhere. She wore an Edwardian dress, veiled hat, shoes, stockings, and carried an umbrella – all entirely grey – even her face was grey! The lady reached her arms out to us and smiled – a particularly sickly smile, I remember – but we were all so scared, we just ran like hell!'

During the Monmouth Rebellion, two rebels were shot to death at the Bull Hotel in East Street. Their unquiet spirits continued to haunt the room where the deed was done, and eventually it was sealed up. The disembodied voice of a child has also been heard calling in the lounge. The 17th-century thatched Bridport Arms hotel also has a spooky reputation, for here pacing footsteps have been heard and an invisible presence enjoys moving and knocking over glasses and turning on and off the beer taps.

Finally, we come to Lyme Regis on the western edge of the Dorset coastline, close to the border with Devon. As mentioned above, Lyme Regis is the place where the Duke of Monmouth landed with his supporters in the hope of wresting the crown from James II. After the planned rebellion failed, Judge Jeffreys held one of his notorious 'Bloody Assizes' here, with the result that twelve men were hanged, guilty or not. One of these now haunts the town. His ghost staggers down Broad Street from the former place of public execution to the famous Cobb breakwater, where a gibbet was set up after the executions. His head is described as lolling horribly on his broken neck.

Judge Jeffreys is also said to haunt the house in which he stayed during the assizes (Jeffreys haunts a remarkable number of places in southern England). This, the Great House, as it was known, is now Boots the Chemist. The Judge's bewigged phantom was believed to stalk the passageways of Great House, literally with blood on his hands (or rather on a blood-stained rag he carries).

The 17th-century Royal Lion Hotel is situated in Broad Street beside the former site of the gallows where the men were hanged after the Monmouth Rebellion. The hotel's ghost manifests as a misty, human-sized shape which brings with it a deathly chill. The apparition comes through the wall from the former place of execution. Often just the cold sensation is felt, sending a shiver up the spine of anyone it passes by.

OUT NOW

BLACK COUNTRY & BIRMINGHAM Ghost Stories
CAMBRIDGESHIRE Ghost Stories
CHESHIRE Ghost Stories
CORNISH Ghost Stories
COTSWOLDS Ghost Stories
CUMBRIAN Ghost Stories
DERBYSHIRE Ghost Stories
ESSEX Ghost Stories
KENT Ghost Stories
LANCASHIRE Ghost Stories
LEICESTERSHIRE Ghost Stories
LONDON Ghost Stories
LONDON UNDERGROUND Ghost Stories
NORTH WALES Ghost Stories
OXFORDSHIRE Ghost Stories
SCOTTISH Ghost Stories
SOUTH WALES Ghost Stories
STAFFORDSHIRE Ghost Stories
SURREY Ghost Stories
SUSSEX Ghost Stories
WELSH CELEBRITY Ghost Stories
YORKSHIRE Ghost Stories

Coming In 2015

HAMPSHIRE & THE ISLE OF WIGHT Ghost Stories
HEREFORDSHIRE Ghost Stories
NORFOLK Ghost Stories
SHROPSHIRE Ghost Stories
SOMERSET Ghost Stories
WARWICKSHIRE Ghost Stories
WILTSHIRE Ghost Stories

BRADWELL BOOKS

See website for more details: **www.bradwellbooks.co.uk**